Contents

Chapter 1

A tricky project

Pedro loved to build. He
helped his father make a tree
house. He helped his grandad
build a fireplace.

One day, his teacher,

Miss Winkle, told the class, "I

have a tricky building project

for you."

"Yay!" yelled Roddy. "I love tricks. I play them on people all the time."

"That's not the sort of *tricky* I mean," said Miss Winkle. "We are going to try to build the tallest tower."

"That's easy!" bragged
Pedro. "All we need are lots
of bricks."

"We are not using bricks,"
said Miss Winkle. "We are
using nineteen paper cups.
You will be working in teams."

Barry and JoJo were on
Katie Woo's team. Sophie
was on Pedro's team. So was
Roddy!

"Watch out!" warned
Katie. "R-O-D-D-Y spells
T-R-O-U-B-L-E."

Chapter 2

Time to build

Miss Winkle told the teams,

"Before you build, you need

to plan."

"I don't need to plan," said

Pedro. "I know what to do."

Pedro began piling up paper cups. He tried to build them high, but the towers kept falling down.

Roddy put four paper cups

on his head.

"Watch out!" he joked. "My

towers are falling down too."

Pedro and Sophie tried
again and again. But the cups
kept falling.

"Oh, boy!" said Pedro.

"I wish we had some bricks."

Then it was break time.

Roddy told Pedro, "Forget
the tower! Let's see who can
do the most handstands. I
know I'll win!"

Roddy flipped upside down

and back again. Pedro tried it.

He kept falling down.

"Watch me and learn,"

said Roddy.

Pedro did watch Roddy.

Then he began thinking.

"That's it!" Pedro yelled.

"You've shown me how to

build the tallest tower."

Chapter 3

The tallest tower

Pedro ran back to the classroom. He said, "Let's put some cups the right way up and some upside down."

Pedro and Sophie began

to build.

"Let me help," said Roddy.

He began piling up the cups.

Their tower got higher and higher. It did not fall! It was the tallest tower!

"Well done!" said Miss

Winkle.

Roddy couldn't stop

smiling. He told Pedro, "I

knew we could do it!"

He gave Pedro a high five.

After school, Pedro said,

"Would you like to help me

fix my tree house?"

"Cool!" said Roddy. "I'll

race you there."

They both won.

About the author

Fran Manushkin is the author
of many popular picture books,
including *Happy in Our Skin*; *Baby,
Come Out!*; *Latkes and Applesauce:
A Hanukkah Story*; *The Tushy
Book*; *Big Girl Panties*; and *Big
Boy Underpants*. Fran writes on
her beloved Mac computer in New York, USA,
without the help of her two naughty cats,
Chaim and Goldy.

About the illustrator

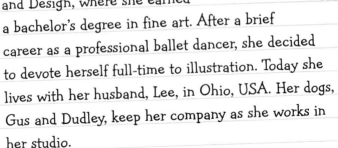

Tammie Lyon began her love of
drawing at a young age while
sitting at the kitchen table with
her dad. She continued her love
of art and eventually attended
the Columbus College of Art
and Design, where she earned
a bachelor's degree in fine art. After a brief
career as a professional ballet dancer, she decided
to devote herself full-time to illustration. Today she
lives with her husband, Lee, in Ohio, USA. Her dogs,
Gus and Dudley, keep her company as she works in
her studio.

Glossary

brag talk about how good you are at something

tower tall structure that is thin in relation to its height

tricky difficult in an unexpected way, needing careful thought or handling

warned told a person about a bad or dangerous thing that could happen

Let's talk

1. Pedro likes to build things. How was his tower building project different from other things he had built?

2. Pedro didn't make a plan, even though his teacher said he should. How might the story have been different if his team had made a plan?

3. Do you think that Pedro and Roddy will be friends now? Why or why not?

Let's write

1. What would you like to build? What supplies would you need? Write a paragraph about it.

2. List five adjectives (describing words) that describe Pedro's team's tower. Then choose one word and write a sentence using it.

3. The students worked in teams. It is important to be a good team member when you are working as a group. Write three tips for being a good team member.

Stack cups for sport!

In this story, Pedro, Sophie and Roddy have to build a tall tower out of paper cups. It was hard, but they did it and won the contest.

But guess what? Stacking and moving cups quickly is an actual sport! It's called Sport Stacking, and competitions are held all over the world. Children are given plastic cups. They must follow strict rules to stack them and move them up and down and back and forth as quickly as possible.

Doing this is tricky! It takes concentration, speed and focus. You can't daydream when you are moving cups around at record speed! Sometimes children work in pairs, which is even trickier!

JOKE AROUND

🔨 What sort of nails do carpenters hate to hammer?
fingernails

🔨 Why did the carpenter stop making wooden cars?
They wooden go.

🔨 "I can cut a piece of wood in half just by looking at it!"
"No way!"
"It's true. I SAW it with my own eyes!"

🔨 Why did the carpenter fall asleep on the job?
He was board.

WITH PEDRO!

What is the tallest tower in town?
the library – it has lots of stories

What animal can jump higher than
Pedro's tower?
any animal – the tower can't jump

THE FUN DOESN'T STOP HERE!

Discover more stories and characters at

www.raintree.co.uk